T0145059

A Wild Hayride

AK Bomar

Illustrated by Sevgi Master

Archway Publishing books may be ordered through booksellers or by contacting:

Archway Publishing
1663 Liberty Drive
Bloomington, IN 47403
www.archwaypublishing.com
844-669-3957

Because of the dynamic nature of the Internet, any web addresses or links contained in this book may have changed since publication and may no longer be valid. The views expressed in this work are solely those of the author and do not necessarily reflect the views of the publisher, and the publisher hereby disclaims any responsibility for them.

ISBN: 978-1-6657-4583-3 (sc)
ISBN: 978-1-6657-4584-0 (e)

Library of Congress Control Number: 2023911275

Print information available on the last page.

Archway Publishing rev. date: 10/13/2023

A WILD HAYRIDE

AK Bomar

Illustrated by Sevgi Master

This book is dedicated to my family,
Bill, Will, Nick, Luke,
Valencia and Aluna.

Edited by: Nicholas Bomar and Luke Bomar

Thank you, Bill, Will, Nick and Luke
for such a wonderful and funny memory.
Our family adventures are my inspiration.

At the annual downtown Christmas Festival, Bill and his family enjoy some warm apple cider and candied pecans as horses dressed like reindeer trot by.

Bill's oldest son, Will, shouts out, "I want to ride that!"

But Will is not yet big enough to ride such a large horse.

Luckily Bill sees the festive hayride passing by the family and is filled
with excitement.
"Now that, you can ride," Bill says.

As Bill and Will walk to the hayride boarding platform, Will's mom, Amelia and his two younger brothers sit on a bench eating their treats and listening to Christmas music.
"Have fun on the hayride!" Amelia yells to Will.

They have no idea the hayride will only be fun for one of them....

WAIT HERE

JOY

Will and Bill are excited to see the hayride arriving. Bill picks up Will and places him on the trailer filled with hay. Surrounded by children, the seats are quickly filled.

Without any open spots, Bill decides to walk behind the hayride to make sure Will is safe on his journey.
The driver yells, "All Aboard!" And the hayride takes off down the road.

The hayride driver speeds up so Bill starts slowly jogging to keep up with them. Bill thinks if the hayride stays in the downtown festival area, he can keep jogging.

Surely the driver will not leave Main Street, Bill hopes.

The hayride turns to exit the festival area and the
driver speeds up getting faster and faster.

Even though the night is cold, Bill begins sweating. The crisp air fills his lungs as Bill sprints down the road to catch the hayride.

As the hayride continues its route and gets farther away, Bill darts through alleys…

He jumps over fences!

He dodges barking dogs… barely!

At one point the hayride turns down a muddy road. Bill is still running behind the hayride trying to keep up but the mud from the dirt road is getting all over his clothes!

Tired, dirty, and sweaty, Bill emerges from some bushes. He can finally see the hayride again down the street. He can hear the children laughing and singing Christmas carols on the hayride. They are having fun!

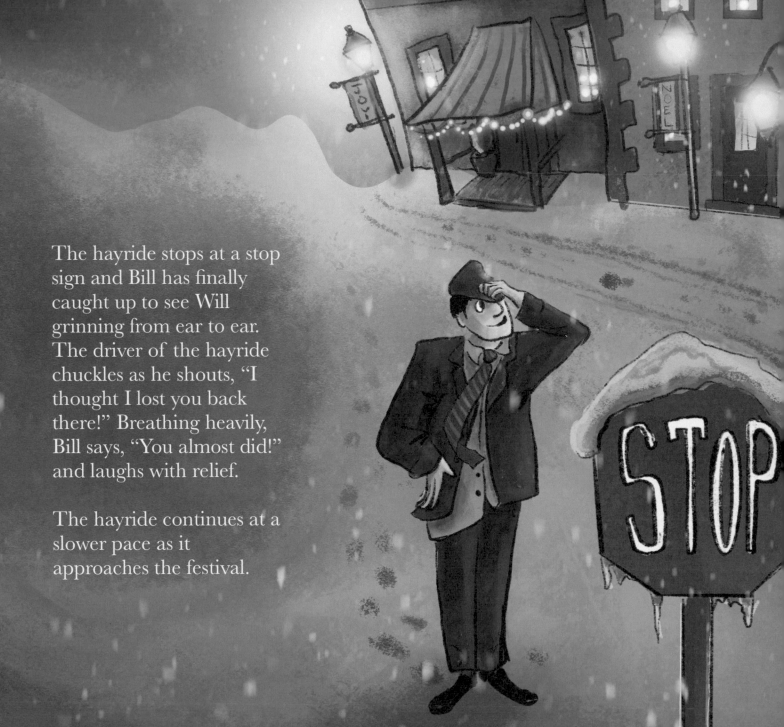

The hayride stops at a stop sign and Bill has finally caught up to see Will grinning from ear to ear. The driver of the hayride chuckles as he shouts, "I thought I lost you back there!" Breathing heavily, Bill says, "You almost did!" and laughs with relief.

The hayride continues at a slower pace as it approaches the festival.

The journey finishes and Will hops off the hayride and excitedly tells his brothers all about the fun ride. "The hayride was so wild!" Will says to his family.

But Amelia curiously smiles at Bill as she notices he looks exhausted and dirty.
Bill says to Amelia, "It definitely was a wild hayride."

The family finishes the festival with popcorn and hot chocolate, smiling and laughing about the wild hayride.

The End!

Glossary

Platform
- a raised floor or
stage

Emerges
-moves out of
something and
comes into view

Darts
- running somewhere
suddenly and
quickly.

Grinning from ear to ear -
to have a large smile;
smile happily

Curiously - wanting to know
or learn something
Exhausted - very tired
Shrugging - the act of
raising one's shoulders
slightly

About the Author

A.K. Bomar is an author who lives with her husband in Tuscaloosa, Alabama. She enjoys hiking and researching her family's genealogy. She grew up in a rural Georgia town and attended high school at Effingham County High. Amelia worked a few years before deciding to attend college at Georgia Southern University where she majored in Sociology. She attended college as a non-traditional, first-generation student and it was at college where she met her husband. She later received her master's degree in Higher Education Administration from the University of Alabama. After serving fifteen years in the field of mental health, she returned to her love of writing. She and her husband have three children and one grandchild.

About the Illustrator

Sevgi Master's global travels and experiences serve as the inspiration for her creative expression. After years of fine art, humanitarian advocacy, and ethical jewelry design, she is pouring her heart into impactful children's books. Her hope is for children (and their parents) to be filled with whimsical wonder & expand the depths of imagination.
 Sevgi is also the Author- Illustrator of *Snuggles and Piggles*, *Beyond Dreams* and *The Well*.

Printed in the United States
by Baker & Taylor Publisher Services